Llama in Pajamas

by Gisela Voss

pictures by
Melissa Sweet

Museum of Fine Arts, Boston

When it's nighttime
in the Andes...

where's my little llama?

Time to come to Mama,

time to put on your pajamas.

Where's my little llama?

Where's my little llama?

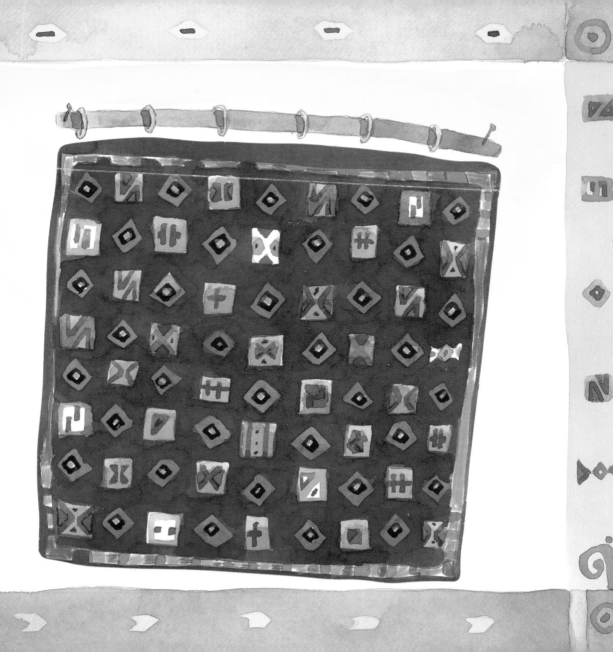

Where's my little llama?

Here's my little llama!

Time to put on
your pajamas.

button,
button

snap
snap

zip

tie, tie, tie

Goodnight my little llama.

Buenas noches, Mama.

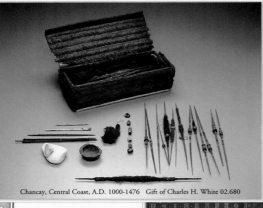

This is a weaver's workbasket, with spindles, bobbins and even some wool.

Chancay, Central Coast, A.D. 1000-1476   Gift of Charles H. White 02.680

This very fine mantle was probably worn by an Incan nobleman.

Neo-Inca Culture About A.D. 1550   Charles Potter Kling Fund 1988.325

Did you know that llama is pronounced YA-ma in Spanish?

The llama is a very important animal to the people who live in the high Andes mountains of South America. Can you find the yarn earring in the mother llama's ear? It shows who owns the llama. The llama carries heavy loads through the mountains. The llama has long, silky hair that can be spun into yarn and woven into warm cloth.

The Department of Textiles and Costumes of the Museum of Fine Arts, Boston has many very old, very beautiful fabrics woven by the Inca and other native people of the Andes region.

If you visit the Museum, you can see many of the things in the little llama's home.